For Trudi – a friend dearly missed
–L.G.

To my dear friend Julie – many thanks
–G.H.

ISBN-10: 0-545-03034-X
ISBN-13: 978-0-545-03034-2

Text copyright © 2007 Lynne Garner
Illustrations copyright © 2007 Gaby Hansen
First published in Great Britain by Piccadilly Press in 2007.
First Scholastic printing, September 2007.
Printed in China by SC (Sang Choy) International Ltd.
Cover illustration © 2007 Gaby Hansen

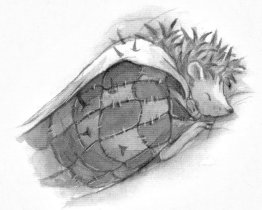

A Book for BRAMBLE

Lynne Garner

Illustrated by Gaby Hansen

SCHOLASTIC INC.

New York Toronto London Auckland Sydney
Mexico City New Delhi Hong Kong Buenos Aires

The leaves
had turned golden
yellow and rusty
red and lay thick on
the ground.

"Winter's coming—time to
hibernate," said Bramble.

"I'll miss you," said Teasel.

"I'll miss you, too,"
replied Bramble,
hugging his friend.

Teasel watched as Bramble and the rest of his family
crept to their nest under the upside-down wheelbarrow.

At dinnertime that evening, Teasel rolled his
roasted hazelnuts and chestnuts around his plate.

"You're missing Bramble, aren't you?"
asked his mother. Teasel nodded sadly.

After dinner, Teasel was bored.

"Why don't you draw a picture?" suggested his mother.

"I know, I'll draw one for Bramble!" said Teasel. "And I'll write to him, too, telling him all about winter. I'll make a book for Bramble."

Teasel got his pencils and a large sketchbook and sat by the roaring fire.

Teasel wrote A BOOK FOR BRAMBLE
in big letters and began.

Dear Bramble,
I'm going to tell you what's happening
while you're asleep. Then we can share
winter when you wake up.

and i will write
very day.

Teasel drew a picture of the upside-down
wheelbarrow where Bramble was now sleeping.
When he had finished, he closed
the book and hid it under his pillow.

The days rolled by
and Teasel still missed
his friend. At the winter
feast there were lots
of delicious things: nuts,
pumpkin pie, and
warm sweet potatoes.

"*If only Bramble was
here,*" thought Teasel.

Teasel sat by the pond, hoping the noise of the party would wake his friend. As he dipped his tail into the cold water and watched the ripples, Mrs. Squirrel came over.

"Teasel, come and join in the games."

"But I want Bramble to be here. He's my BEST friend," said Teasel.

"I know, dear, but you can share the fun with him in your book."

Teasel was very tired after the party,
but he had lots to write in Bramble's book that day.

We made a bonfire.
The flames were
red and yellow
and warmed our
cold noses.

Mrs. Squirrel hid
nuts, which we had to find.
It was so much fun.
I wish you'd been there!

The weather grew colder and colder. One day Teas
found the puddles on the path had turned to ice.
"Come skating with us," called his brother, Sedg

That night, Teasel wrote:

We tied walnutshells on our feet
and skated all day. I kept falling down,
but I got better by the end!

The days became colder still.
When Teasel looked out of the window
one morning, everything seemed
to be covered in a thick white blanket.

"It's snowing! It's snowing!" he shouted, running into the kitchen.

"We know," said his sister, Meadow. "We're going to play in the snow after breakfast!"

"Bramble would love this," said Teasel as he gathered another paw full of snow. "I do miss him."

"I know. Let's make a snow-hedgehog in his honor," replied Sedge.

That night, Teasel drew a picture of the snow-hedgehog for Bramble, and wrote:

It was huge. I wish you could have seen it. When we finished, we had a snowball fight. Then Sedge broke off some icicles and we had ice pops.

Teasel was having lots of fun that winter—
but still he missed Bramble.

Slowly, spring came.
Flowers poked through the ground,
and the sun grew stronger.
Teasel knew that Bramble would soon
wake up. He took a basket of
nuts with him when he went to the
wheelbarrow. Bramble would
be hungry after his long sleep.

At last Teasel heard shuffling coming from the wheelbarrow.
One by one, Bramble's family crept out into the sunlight.

Finally Bramble emerged, yawning and stretching. "Bramble Teasel shouted, running to greet his friend. "I MISSED you!"

"I missed you, too!" said Bramble. "I know
I did because I dreamed about you."

"I made a book for you, so
that we could share winter,"
said Teasel. "Do you want
to see it?"

"Oh, yes! I've always wanted
to know what winter was like!"
said Bramble.

And the two friends sat by
the pond together as
Bramble began to read,

"Dear Bramble . . ."